YOUNG MINDS, BIG CELEBRATIONS

AF518022

Authors Tree®
PUBLISHING

YOUNG MINDS, BIG CELEBRATIONS

Copyright @ 2024 by Khushi Hinduja

All rights reserved. No part of this publication may be reproduced, stored in a retrieval system or transmitted in whole or part including photocopying, recording or other electronic or mechanical methods without the prior written permission of the publisher.

Cover designed by **Authors Tree Publishing**, image used from free stock library.

ISBN: 978-93-94807-98-3
India: INR 399/-
Outside India: $ 5.99 USD

Authors Tree®
PUBLISHING

Authors Tree Publishing
W/13, Aman Vihar, BSP
Pin: 495001
Call: +91 9109886656
www.authorstree.com
First Edition. 2024

This book has been published with all reasonable efforts taken to make the material error-free after the consent of the author. No part of this book shall be used, reproduced in any manner whatsoever without written permission from the author, except in the case of brief quotations embodied in critical articles and reviews. The author of this book is solely responsible and liable for its content including but not limited to the views, representations, descriptions, statements, information, opinions and references ["content"]. The content of this book shall not constitute or be construed or deemed to reflect the opinion or expression of the publisher or editor. Neither the publisher nor editor endorse or approve the content of this book or guarantee the reliability, accuracy or completeness of the content published herein and do not make any representations or warranties of any kind, express or implied, including but not limited to the implied warranties of merchantability, fitness for a particular purpose. the publisher and editor shall not be liable whatsoever for any errors, omissions, whether such errors or omissions result from negligence, accident, or any other cause or claims for loss or damages of any kind, including without limitation, indirect or consequential loss or damage arising out of use, inability to use, or about the reliability, accuracy or sufficiency of the information contained in this book.

Printed In India

YOUNG MINDS, BIG CELEBRATIONS

Happiness Crafted by Kids

Compiled By

Khushi Hinduja

Table of Contents

Preface

Greetings, Dear Readers!

We extend a warm welcome to our captivating journey within the pages of "Young Minds, Big Celebrations."

Celebration is like finding treasures in everyday moments. It's the happy dance when you see a rainbow after rain or catch fireflies at dusk. Celebrating is about giggles with friends, making funny faces with family, and feeling the warm sun on your face. It's the excitement of learning something new, the cozy feeling of bedtime stories, and the joy of helping others. Celebrating life means cherishing the little moments that fill your heart with warmth, like when a pet curls up beside you or you share a secret laugh with a friend. It's about making ordinary moments extraordinary!

In a world dominated by treasures, we aim to unravel the enchantment of those delightful moments that exist beyond the physical, like the quiet whispers of a gentle breeze, the comfort of a supportive friend, and the laughter that lingers in the air long after it's gone.

Within the pages of this book, you'll encounter a lot of narratives, each a testament to the magic of intangible things. We want to share stories that celebrate the unseen beauty in everyday life, from the simple pleasure of learning something new to the great impact of a kind word or gesture. These intangible celebrations are the threads that bind us together, making new connections.

Our mission is to inspire you to recognize and appreciate the little moments that often go unnoticed. We want to encourage you to pause, reflect, and find joy in the many aspects of your journey through life. It's in these invisible celebrations that we discover the true essence of happiness.

Throughout these pages, you'll find not just stories but also reflections and creative expressions designed to open your eyes to the small wonders around you. Our hope is that you'll be inspired to embrace the magic in the unseen moments that shape your world.

So, young readers, come along, on this extraordinary journey into the celebration of various things. Let these stories serve as a reminder that joy can be found in the simplest, often invisible, moments of life. May this book spark your curiosity and fill your hearts with the warmth of unseen celebrations.

Happy reading, happy exploring, and, above all, happy celebrating!

- **Khushi Hinduja**

(Parenting and Teen Success Coach)

About The Compiler

Khushi Hinduja is an Author of book **Gen-X Parenting - Traditional Wisdom to Raise your Supa Kids** and also compiler of the book **I See Spring** which is widely available on authorstree.com & amazon/flipkart. She has curated a journal named Joy of Journaling for children.

She is on a mission to spread happiness in life of parents and children. She is also a DMIT Consultant, Parenting Coach and Keynote Speaker invited as Guest Speaker at various events.

Awarded –

- India's 100 Women Achiever 2023
- HerStory Times Inspiration Award
- XtraOrdiNaari 2022

Author

Nihaal Sylva

Nihaal Sylva is an 11-year-old author from Solihull, England. He loves athletics, football and art. His dream is to play professional football and, in some way, this story 'You Can Create Miracles' is a journey of his own life that he wants to share and inspire all who read it. He is always striving to help his friends and family change their attitudes and transform their days from bad to good ones.

1

You Can Create Miracles!

By Nihaal Sylva

There was once a boy named Jake Jones and he wasn't any other ordinary kid; he could create miracles. Jake lived in a normal family with his, Mom, Dad and little brother, Henry. They lived in Stourbridge, England in a flat. His Mom worked as a teacher and his Dad was a businessman. He didn't get much time with his family, because his parents were always busy, striving hard to make a living. Jake was a short boy with ocean-blue eyes and hair smoother than a feather.

He had a few friends because other children always bullied him for his lack of height. He was really smart and intelligent and answered every question in class. But the one thing he was really good at was, FOOTBALL! He was crazy about it. Especially the team Manchester United and he watched every game and knew every player. Ask him a football question and he would know the answer without hesitation. Every day he finished his homework, rushed to the park and practiced his football skills. He played for a team called Stourbridge FC. His position in the team was left winger.

The only thing that bothered him was that he couldn't score a single goal for his team, despite being such a talented player. He started having doubts about playing the game. He kept on saying that he wasn't good enough and that just made it worse. (*Why do you think it made it worse? Is it because our words create our thoughts which consequently create our actions and reality?)*

After a few weeks, it just got to him and he couldn't hold it in anymore, so he told his mother he was feeling depressed and was flooded with tears. So, his mother told him about her past and her own story. She told him that before she became a teacher, she found it difficult to get a job it was that point of time in her life where she NEEDED a job the most. Until one day when she went to church and from that day her life changed. The priest said, "My dear child, you should ask for whatever you want before you go to sleep every night and also believe that you have already received it". So, she followed his instructions and after a few days, she met a friend randomly in the grocery shop. This man asked her "Do you want to be a teacher in my school as there currently is a vacancy?" and without hesitation she said "Yes!". She was amazed by what the priest had taught her. Jake questioned his mother "If this could happen to you does that mean that it can happen to me too?" She nodded her head and both of them had huge smiles on their faces. Jake wiped away his tears and got ready for his new journey with a refreshed mind. So, from that night itself, he followed the steps that his mum guided him with. Everyone knew that there was a BIG change in Jake he was happy once again. He had a renewed hope in himself and he was determined to achieve his goal.

Next Saturday, Jake prayed so much that night and fell asleep but his dream wasn't a good one it was a terrible one. In his dream, he was playing a match when suddenly he got seriously injured. The opponent went in for a slide tackle but it caught Jake in the back of his leg and he fractured it. In the morning, his mom woke up to find Jake crying in his room. He explained his dream to his mother and she tried to comfort him. At this time, Jake was too upset to care about what she said but then something they did changed both of them and that SOMETHING was called the blessing ball of light. *(You can try it too by YouTubing 'Blessing ball of light').*

At first it was too crazy to believe! His mum explained how it worked "Close your eyes and imagine you are holding a ball and that you are gathering up all the light from all the galaxies in the whole universe and when you collect it, label it with your name and ask for something that you desire. When you have finished doing that, let it up into the air believing you have received all that you want. Jake and his mom did it together and when they did it, they felt a touch like no other. It was like another World, a blissful one they were both contented now. Jake was ready to score that goaltoday. He was determined to do it and no one was going to get in his way. As his dad was driving him to his match Jake was so excited to score the goal in the game. His dad gave him some winning game strategies and motivated him. The day had come to score the goal.

The match kicked off at sharp 10 a.m. Jake got off to a rough start but did not give up. Twenty minutes into the game he got the ball, dribbled past both the defenders, shot it outside of the box and went right at the back of the net! Hurrah! Everyone cheered with excitement as it was an outstanding goal. The next possession, Jake's teammate launched the ball up falling right into Jake's feet, he took a touch and boom it went right into the top, right corner. Gooooaaaalll! In the second half, Jake remembered he watched one of his favourite, football player's goals right before the match and he tried to do what the player did. It was a corner for Jake's team his mate crossed the ball into the box perfectly for Jake and he kicked it up in the air again and did a backflip into the air. He buried it into the net scoring not only his first goal but his first hat trick. It was magnificent to watch.

Later on in life, Jake became one of the best football players in history and everyone looked up to him as a superstar. But the one person he thanked the most was his mother for encouraging him and teaching him how to create miracles for himself.

Always remember in life, you should always believe in yourself and remain positive no matter what the situation. If you are negative, you are only telling the universe that you don't deserve it. So, keep believing and keep creating miracles and the life that you want because you deserve the best!

THERE IS SOMETHING GOOD IN *everyday*

Today I am grateful for...

Author

Pia Hinduja

Pia Hinduja is a 14-year-old author from Mumbai, Maharashtra. She is a Rhythmic Gymnast and studies in Lilavatibai Podar High School, ISC. She is an avid reader. She enjoys dancing and quilling. She is learning Kathak which is a classical dance form. During her free time she enjoys listening to music and she loves to spend time with her family.

2

From Setbacks to Success

By Pia Hinduja

As ***Barack Obama*** **quotes and I write,** ***"You can't let your failures define you. You have to let your failures teach you."***

I still remember that day, it is so crystal clear in my mind as if it was just yesterday. My mother enrolled me for rhythmic gymnastics at Premier Rhythmic Gymnastics Academy.

I was extremely young when I visited the center. I was so mesmerized with the way the girls were practicing. They were doing cart-wheels, splits, rolls, stretching exercises, and what not. I was engrossed watching them. My mother registered me very happily for the batch which was thrice a week for an hour. Initially I was taught simple exercises, jumps, skips but after few months I was taught techniques to increase my strength.

My parents were happy that I was away from gadgets and spent time in a very constructive way whereas other children of my age used to watch cartoon network and YouTube channels. Life was going smoothly in a regular routine until one day my Senior Head Coach told my mother that it was time for me to shift for the advanced level. Now my training was to be continued a little more away from home. My mother was extremely enthusiastic, hence, she instantly agreed.

I started my advanced training, under the guidance of Mrs. Varsha Upadhye (Senior Head Coach), my coaches Kshipra Joshi, Sadichchha Kulkarni and Sanjeevani Purnapatre, (my respected Tais who are still mentoring me.)

Since then, every day, my life has given me new challenges and every single time I try to accept these challenges and put my best foot forward to solve them. However, I never get disheartened when I am unable to achieve success. Instead, I embrace my failure and celebrate it. I learn something new, each time I fail and this makes me stronger from within.

With each new challenge in life, I need to step up my game and try harder each time. All my failures help me to grow fearless and face my challenges with vigor and achieve higher goals and success. And so, today I would like to share my life story, my personal experience on how I embraced failure and how it helped me to become what I am today.

I am an international level Rhythmic Gymnast and I have been playing this sport since I was 3 years old. Rhythmic Gymnastics is a sport which includes various apparatus like ball, hoop, clubs, ribbon combined with dance movements and music. We need to have good core strength and a flexible body to perform our routines.

From the very beginning, I was struggling to increase my flexibility. I was not as flexible as my other friends. I had to work really hard to improve my routines. Each time I tried something new, I had to take a step back because of lack of a flexible body. In order to achieve success I took various steps to work on my weakness. My coaches trained and mentored me with rigorous stretching exercises. Though it made my eyes water, I did it with a positive mindset and a brave smile. After a lot of hard-work, dedication, patience and perseverance I was able to overcome my failure and stretch myself beyond my limits. I was finally moving closer to my goal.

As time passed by, I got an opportunity to perform at a competitive level. Being the youngest in the batch with very little experience, I did not perform well in the first few competitions. This did not dishearten me. In fact, I learnt so many other things during that time. I became more independent and was able to make quick decisions for myself. I understood that working hard is the stepping stone to success. I started analyzing my drawbacks. I worked for long hours and spent most of my time towards this sport.

Finally, during one of the competitions, I performed extremely well and all my efforts paid off. I become Maharashtra State Champion not once but twice. I also got an opportunity to represent our country at various international competitions where I won medals and made my coaches, school and parents proud of me. Infact I even got an opportunity to perform in front of our honorable Prime Minister Mr. Narendra Modi, Chief Minister of Maharashtra, Deputy

Chief Minister of Maharashtra, Sports Minister of India during the opening ceremony of the 27th National Youth Festival.

When I look back at those days, I smile at the innocence of that little girl who enrolled in fun gymnastics not aware that one day it would change her fate by giving her recognition at the academy and at her school. Her efforts had given wings to her dreams. And today that same little girl with the same little innocence, promises herself to never let her spirit die no matter how tough the situation is.

It's been more than 11 years now, but I feel truly blessed to have my coaches in my life. They have always hugged me, taken good care of me, have given me the strength to face my fears, stood by me and without them this would have not been possible.

In the end, I would like to send a message that everyone must learn from their failures if they want to conquer success. True happiness lies not in winning, but the journey, which shapes the character of your personality and leads you to success. With all the failures that we face, we must learn from them and bounce back harder to achieve great limits.

I would like to spare a moment to acknowledge all my coaches for their unwavering mentorship which they have given me throughout my journey in this sport. I would also like to thank my respected school faculty for their unconditional support and share my heartfelt gratitude to my peers who have wiped my tears during my emotional ups and downs and they have been my solid rock in all phases of my life.

Special thank you to my family who have always encouraged and stood beside me like a pillar through my entire life.

CHEERS!

Quote of the day

3

Race to Victory

By Pia Hinduja

Born with a congenital ailment that affected Emma's lower limbs, she was a great athlete who had to overcome challenges that would have discouraged many. But Emma came out as more than simply a Paralympian—she inspired everyone facing difficulties by serving as a constant reminder that the real test of a person is their capacity to overcome hardship.

Emma's natural love of movement brought her into athletics from an early age. She showed great zeal for life that broke limitations imposed by her physical condition from a young age. Her parents, encouraged her to explore different avenues.

It was during a local Paralympic event that Emma first discovered wheelchair racing. The speed, the adrenaline, and the sheer freedom of racing on the track resonated with her in a way that went beyond the physical. For Emma, it was a revelation—a moment when she realized that her body, though different, could still be a vessel for strength and achievement.

However, the path to Paralympic glory was not very easy. Emma faced not only the physical challenges of mastering a sport but also the societal misconceptions surrounding disability. She encountered scepticism from peers and, at times, even misguided advice about what she could or couldn't achieve. Yet, every raised eyebrow, every doubtful glance only fuelled Emma's determination to prove that her abilities far outweighed her perceived limitations.

Her training began daily early mornings at the track, countless hours in the gym, and a rigorous schedule of strengthening exercises became Emma's routine. The track became her proving ground, a space where she could change the physical boundaries imposed by her condition and redefine what was possible.

She met fellow athletes who shared similar journeys of overcoming adversity, forming bonds that went beyond the competition. They became a support system, a source of inspiration, and a reminder that she was not alone in her quest to break barriers. They realized challenges were not obstacles but opportunities for growth.

Emma's breakthrough came during a national competition, where she not only won the race but shattered records in the process. Her triumph echoed through the sports world, challenging perceptions and redefining expectations. The victory, however, was not just about the medals; it was about the resilience that had brought her to that moment, the countless hours of sweat and determination that had paved the way for success.

She was invited as a guest speaker at schools, engaged with community programs, and became a role model for aspiring athletes facing similar challenges. Emma's message was simple yet powerful: disability does not define a person's potential, and with the right support and opportunities, anyone could achieve greatness.

Her story resonated and it became a ray of hope for individuals facing diverse challenges—whether physical, emotional, or societal. Emma's journey taught us that the human spirit, when ignited by passion could soar to unimaginable heights. She became a living example of the idea that limitations are often products of our minds, and with the right mindset, we can redefine what's possible.

As the Paralympic Games approached, Emma faced a new set of challenges. The pressure to perform on the global platform, along with the lot of expectations, could have been overwhelming. Yet, Emma approached it with the same grace and determination that had defined her journey so far. She saw the Games not just as a personal triumph but as an opportunity to share her message of empowerment.

On the day of her Paralympic race, the stadium buzzed with anticipation. The crowd of supporters waving banners and flags, felt the electricity in the air. Emma, focused and composed, approached the starting line with confidence. Her burst of energy left spectators breathless.

Competing against elite athletes from around the world was not easy. Yet, with each turn of the wheel, she demonstrated determination that had become an integral part of her character.

In the final stretch of the race, Emma moved ahead, crossing the finish line with a triumphant smile. The stadium erupted in cheers as she basked in the glory of her victory. The medal around her neck wasn't just a symbol of triumph but it was also dedicated to those who dared to dream.

Emma's journey, from a small town to the global stage, served as a reminder that inspiration could be found in every place. Her story encouraged us to look beyond challenges, and recognize the potential that is in each individual.

Even after her Paralympic victory, Emma continued to contribute in sports and society. She touched lives of countless individuals who found peace and motivation in her story. Emma's journey wasn't just about overcoming physical challenges; it was about breaking down barriers, challenging stereotypes, and redefining societal norms.

Life has given me
Let's write down 3 things which you appreciate from Life
01.
02.
03.

Author

Smaya Bhalotia

Smaya Bhalotia is a 10-year-old author from Mumbai, Maharastra. She studies in S.V.K.M JV Parekh International School. She got inspired to write her book during school vacations when her mom encouraged her to write poetries and stories. Soon, she found herself engrossed and interested in all this. It revealed her inner talent. The sessions with Ms. Khushi Ma'am were amazing and she was so polite and gracious throughout all the sessions. This helped her to become an author.

4

Tale of two Sisters

By Smaya Bhalotia

Siblings share a relation of love and hate.
But there were 2 sisters who were great.

Through hard work and persistence
They got greatness and excellence.

Throughout their life, with progress
In a short span of time, they got success.

It was a splendid evening. The sun was setting, the moon was about to rise. The sky was filled with vibrant colors of reds and pinks. Mr. and Mrs. Jaffer were at the dining table with their children, Aisha, Inaya and Ahsan. It was winter time and the outside temperature was 6^0 C. The family had a tiny little bonfire in the corner of the gigantesque house to keep them warm.

They were relishing their hot bowl of soup along with mashed potatoes and seasoned turkey.

Aisha, who was the elder daughter, had long silky hair and a ravishing face. Her most-liked colors were purple and blue. She was gracious, helpful, and caring by nature, which made her an emotional person. Aisha loved singing and dancing. Her favorite K-Pop band was BTS.

Inaya, on the other hand was the second child who loved a K-Pop group named Blackpink. She used to listen to their songs all day long and with a carefree attitude she would almost forget that there were some other crucial things to be focused on. Inaya was a loveable, graceful and a straight -forward child. She was more of a practical person.

Ahsan was a little naughty during his childhood but he was a great listener. He grasped everything he heard or saw because he was intelligent. Ahsan was pampered all the time because he was the youngest of all the siblings. His bonding with the family was close and everyone loved him.

All of them were comfortably seated in their chairs. There was silence in the room as they were quietly eating their feast, until Aisha spoke. She was waiting for the right time as she wanted to discuss about something significant. She uttered hesitatingly, "The food tastes amazing. Mom, would you kindly pass me some more soup?" Her mom could understand her emotion and while passing her the soup bowl, she asked, "Child, do you want to say something?"

Aisha and Inaya looked at each other and this time Inaya asked, "Mom, dad, now that we are soon going to complete our higher education, we would like to talk about our future plans." Mr. Jaffer asked in a concerned tone, "What would you both like to do?"

Aisha cleared her throat and said, "We both would like to follow our passion. Inaya wants to complete her Masters while I would like to pursue engineering. What do you think about it?" Mr. and Mrs. Jaffer took a few minutes to discuss amongst themselves. They were joyous that their daughters had become independent enough to take a stand for themselves, so they decided to give them a green signal to follow what they wished for. Aisha and Inaya felt lucky because they had such supportive parents.

Few months passed by. Aisha and Inaya continued following their dreams and from time to time they also gave their younger brother valuable advice on how he could work harder and better to make a good future for himself.

During their childhood, they had lots of fun. They cherished every single moment. The bond between the two sisters was extremely close. They were just like best friends. In school, if anyone quarreled with any of them, they always stood together and supported each other.

Their parents were ambitious individuals who loved their jobs and were very dedicated towards it. Mr. Jaffer was a cardiologist. He used to consult patients and treat them at a clinic. He earned a lot of money and saved it by investing it in shares and bonds. Mrs. Jaffer, was a renowned author. She was writing her 4th book that eventually got published and once again became the best seller in the world. Though they were busy, they loved their children and spent quality time with them.

The family was from India. Initially when they had Aisha and Inaya they decided to move to USA as they thought their children would have better learning opportunities in a foreign country. Once they settled down in USA, they had an adorable baby boy.

Aisha and Inaya were now young adults where they were beginning their career journey. Aisha had started her own center in the field of Science and Technology where she planned to build robots that could help the society. Whereas Inaya was in the initial phase where she would soon commence her career in the field of teaching English.

After few years Aisha and Inaya were successful in their respective fields. They were so lively that they capered with enthusiasm. The two sisters were now well-known as the 'Lead Girls' in their community, who helped everyone. They were on a mission to make the world a better place to live.

Days passed by. Later, they both, along with their parents travelled back to India in Mumbai, which was their hometown. Inaya continued teaching children and adults to develop their English language skills and built a platform where they could enhance their public speaking skills too. On the other hand, Aisha helped numerous people to gain knowledge in science and technology which helped them to create new inventions for the betterment of the people in the society.

After a few years, they both got whole lot of recognition and received numerous awards for serving the nation.

That was a great way to live life!
They celebrated life, by giving glee to the society.

Moral of the story:

Success is not always about greatness. It is about consistency. Consistent hard work leads to success. The only thing standing between us and outrageous success is our procrastination and laziness. When we overcome this challenge, 'Greatness' will take place on its own.

Stay away from those people who try to perish your ambitions. Small minds will always try to do that, however, people who love you or like you will always boost your confidence that will make you feel that you can be great too.

A little more hard work, a little more endeavor and what looks like a horrendous failure may turn into glorious success.

BEST PART ABOUT HAVING A

Family

Author

Nysha Nagpal

Nysha Nagpal is a 10-year-old author from Mumbai, Maharastra. She studies in Don Bosco International School. She loves singing. She enjoys shopping & playing. She wants to become an Author so she can share her experience with other children and the entire world.

5

Triumphs and Trophies

By Nysha Nagpal

Let me begin my story by introducing myself. My name is Nysha Nagpal. I am a tan girl with short hair. I like to go to school and enjoy making new friends. I love sports. I relish good home cooked food and sometimes junk food. My hobbies include learning new things.

My motto in life, "It doesn't matter if you fall down, it's whether you get back up." by *Michael Jordon*.

Few years back when I got admission in Don Bosco International School, I was introduced to various extra-curricular activities like drawing, yoga, skating. During my school hours I was taken to the school grounds where I got an opportunity to play different kind of sports like judo, hockey, hand-ball, athletics and basket-ball and foot-ball. The first ever sport which I tried was Judo but then I lost interest in it as it was an individual sport and decided to switch to another sport. I used to thoroughly enjoy these activities because my coaches not only guided me but most importantly made me enjoy what I was doing. On other regular school days I used to feel a little lazy to go to school but days when we had sports I used to look forward going to school.

Few weeks passed by and we were done with our class assessments. Our class teacher announced that there would be competitions in various fields where we could participate and a circular from school was sent home. The list included mono-acting, poetry writing, debate, fancy dress, poster-making and many more. As soon as I reached home my mother asked me, "Nysha, how was school today?" This was a daily ritual question from her to me and as usual she was expecting the same old 'not-interested' expression from me. But that day was different. That afternoon I was so excited to share the note stapled in the school diary which mentioned about the events and competitions. I told my mother that I wanted to enroll and register myself for the basketball team as it was my favorite game.

Initially my mother was a little hesitant as she did not have much knowledge about the sport. No one from our family had ever participated in these kind of games. But I somehow convinced her to come to school with me and have a word with my sports teacher.

The next day when she met my coaches, they explained to my mother that I was really good at basketball and they made sure, she filled the form given by my class teacher. Now I was a part of the team. I was so happy and was on cloud nine, while my mother looked nervous. We came home and did a little bit of research about the sport. While doing so, I got really inspired by Michael Jordon. His positive attitude inspired me. When I read his quotes it motivated me. I decided that I have to do something in my life and contribute to my school.

After my school hours, I was told to wait back for extra coaching. When I started warm-ups and practiced with my team, I understood the importance of team work. I learnt that working as a team can be beneficial in so many ways. It helped to find solutions to problems, built leadership qualities, developed confidence. Before, I was facing difficulty in shooting and crossovers but I never gave up. Finally with regular practice I learnt the technique. My coaches told me that I had improved my game and was now good at dribbles and shooting.

My mother also started taking extra efforts to cook nutritious meals for me which included dals, roasted nuts and millets. I became disciplined and started sleeping on time. I understood the importance of taking proper rest to stay focused and energized during my practices.

My grandmother too started giving me warm oil massages so that I was relaxed after long working hours. I felt a sense of responsibility. With the kind of support my family, class teacher and coaches were giving I became more aware about myself. I did not waste time like other children. My team-mates too, made sure to put in 100% efforts to play during practice so that we were prepared during the competition.

Finally the day arrived when we were going to play our first interschool competition. That day my friends were little nervous but I felt very confident. So before we began I gave them a tight hug to help them calm down. Towards the end of the competition I made my first goal. My team won the competition. I was so delighted. By the time I reached home at night, I was so tired that I immediately went to sleep.

The next day when my mother woke me up from sleep, she showed me the newspaper which mentioned that our school had won the competition and my name was written below our group photograph. This came as a pleasant surprise to all of us. That day my family celebrated my victory.

The next day when I went to school, I thanked my school Principal and class teacher. I was grateful to my coaches who identified my skills and helped me with my struggles to achieve success. We even lost a couple of matches but that failure did not stop me. Later, I also got selected for MSSA, ISSO and other competitions. I am now planning to continue this journey and represent school all my life.

Things you wish to start in the morning

☐

☐

☐

Author

Poorvika Agrawal

Poorvika Agrawal is a 9-year-old author from Solapur, Maharastra. She studies in Indian Model International School. She enjoys reading good books and her sessions with Ms. Khushi Ma'am were very interesting.

6

Rise of an Entrepreneur

By Poorvika Agrawal

Parth was a boy who was born in a middle-class family. His mother worked as a house-helper and his father was a station master. He was well-built, had golden brown hair, big black eyes. He had broad shoulders. Most of the time he was dressed in shabby clothes. At his home they ate simple food which included *jowar bhakri*, dal, rice and one vegetable. Parth lived in a chawl. His family included, grandparents, parents and cousins. Parth used to begin his day by eating a banana, sometimes egg and a glass of milk. He started schooling when he was 6 years old but his parents did not have enough money to send him to a private school. Though Parth did not always get what he wanted, he was still happy with what he had.

Parth was a very bright and matured child. As he grew much older, he realized it was time for him to support his parents who were slowly growing old. His father was about to get retired in a couple of years and mother too reduced work as it was getting difficult to manage home. So he decided to look for a small job which he could manage along with his studies. He went to a few shops but nobody supported him. Few shopkeepers yelled at him, while, others insulted him. But this did not affect him. He did not give up.

After few days he managed to get a part time job at a tea shop. After school hours he used to directly go to the shop. During weekends he went there from morning to evening. The owner of the shop, Anandji, was also a very kind man. He liked Parth because he used to work really hard and did not take a single leave. He used to help Parth by giving him extra bonus on occasions. Anandji encouraged him to learn different other things. He gave him newspaper to read, then during free time, they discussed about various topics which helped Parth to increase his knowledge. Anandji treated him like one of his own.

Parth did not have many friends so even he used to enjoy spending time at the tea shop. Nobody in school spoke to him because he was from a poor family. But he was very good in academics and all the teachers supported him by giving him extra time to clear his doubts. Now his daily routine was to go to school during the day, then go to work, eat dinner and after that he studied at night below street lights because there was no space at home. He had few friends from the chawl. But most of the time, he used to feel sad at school as his classmates avoided him, did not eat meals with him, no one played with him.

Parth was a very good athlete. He won many medals and certificates for the school. He was inspired by none other than Milkha Singh. One important value which he learnt from him was to be kind to others, be humble, respect competitors, no matter who they were.

After few years, when Parth was in higher grades he got an opportunity to partner with another classmate, named Mahesh for an inter-school science project. Mahesh was a year younger to Parth. They won first place for this and got appreciated by the school Principal. From then, they both became best friends.

Mahesh belonged to a well to do family. His father was a C.E.O. of a multinational company and his mother was a socialite. One day Mahesh invited Parth to his home to spend time with him. Mahesh lived in a big grand house. Parth knew this and was hesitant to go but Mahesh insisted. As soon as Parth reached he was extremely surprised to see such a neat and clean house. Mahesh's father was busy and was travelling during that time for an important client meeting, while his mother was out for a function. They both spent good quality time with each other at home. Mahesh missed his parents. Parth started coming more frequently at his house.

One evening when Parth came to visit Mahesh, his father was sitting in the living room. He was having his tea. He asked Mahesh about Parth. Mahesh introduced him by saying he was his best friend and told him how they met. Mahesh's dad was pretty impressed by Parth's presence of mind. Even after many months, his dad remembered him.

It was time for them now to seek admission in college. They had to focus on their ambitions. Then they graduated from college. Parth wanted to become a businessman and Mahesh wanted to become a singer. As soon as Mahesh's dad came to know about this, he called them. He wanted to tell them that he was proud of them as they both had decided to pursue their passion.

The next day he called Parth to his office. He immediately offered him a job in his company. Parth was so excited that he instantly agreed. Seeing him work so hard, Parth was given a promotion in a short span of time. On the other hand, Mahesh became a successful world famous singer and performed at many international stage shows.

Time passed by, Mahesh's dad was about to retire in a few weeks. He wanted Parth to take over his company. Parth was speechless and promised to take the company to new heights. One evening, Parth and Mahesh decided to meet over dinner. That night they did not sleep. They remembered their old days, laughed out loud and celebrated their success as they both achieved their dreams.

1 THING THAT YOU WOULD LIKE TO CHANGE ABOUT YOURSELF

"Be gentle with yourself."

7

An Exciting Family Vacation

By Poorvika Agrawal

It was 2021. Aditi a young, intelligent girl who was cute wore spectacles and had wavy hair. She had medium height. She was afraid of insects. She was a very independent child who knew how to look after herself. Her hobby was to paint. Aditi liked playing tennis. But at home, she enjoyed playing with her soft toys, blocks and toy cars. She lived in a joint family. They resided in Mumbai. Her family members loved her very much and took great care of her. Aditi's grandfather and both parents were doctors. She had many friends.

It was Aditi's 7th birthday. She was very happy and excited. She was looking forward to celebrate her birthday in a special way with friends. That day after the cake was cut and all her friends went home. Her mother called her. She gave Aditi a hug and told her that she would soon become an elder sister. Aditi jumped with joy. After a few days, on 12th January, Aditi's mother gave birth to a baby boy. When Aditi went to visit her mother at the hospital, her grandmother told Aditi to hold the little one in her arms. Aditi smiled and kissed him.

After four days, Aditi's mother was discharged. She was coming home. Aditi and her grandmother planned a surprise welcome party for them. Very close family members were invited. After few days, when everything settled down, they organized a small naming ceremony for the baby boy. Initially they were planning to name him Lithvik, but finally they named him Aryan.

Aditi loved Aryan very much. She was very attached to him. She played with him, took him to the garden, fed him his meals. She looked after him with great care and affection. Aryan too like Aditi, was chubby and cute. But he was naughty.

After few years, when Aditi turned nine and Aryan was two, they went for a vacation with family to Lucknow. Over there, they planned to visit the most popular amusement park. As soon as they reached, the place was filled with children. There they had lots of fun. They sat on the roller coaster, bumper cars, scrambler and the carousel. They ate some yummy cotton cadies which melted in their mouth. They also saw a magic show where the magician performed different tricks. They also visited various food stalls where they ate variety of food, some game stalls where they played with rings, threw balls, bought colorful heart shaped balloons and blew bubbles with the bubble-maker and burst them.

When they were enjoying themselves, there was a drastic change in the weather. This was absolutely unexpected but nature had some different plans. Suddenly it became dark and it started drizzling. There was a strong gush of wind and within few seconds, it poured heavily. People began to run to find shelter. There was a lot of hustle and bustle around the place. The organizers had to stop the rides, the food stalls shut down. But the organizing committee was very helpful. They assured the crowd that everything would be fine. They arranged for umbrellas and started transferring people to another place where they could be safe. During this chaos, an 8 year old child fell and got hurt.

Aditi immediately rushed to pick him up. The boy's mother thanked Aditi for helping him.

It was 4pm. The rain too stopped. Things were coming back to normal. People were out in the open. They played the music again and by 5:45pm the entire place lit up with amazing lights. Later that evening, they also had a wonderful fire work show which was mesmerizing. At 10pm Aditi along with her family went back to the hotel. Aditi went to sleep as she had a tiring day.

The next morning when they woke up, they planned to visit a nearby zoo. As soon as they reached the main gate, they saw a small queue. They had to wait for a few minutes to purchase the tickets. Inside the zoo, they saw many animals like elephants, deer, bears, hyena, peacocks and tigers. The bear was sleeping. Two baby elephants were eating sugarcane and few bigger elephants were standing under a huge shade. But when the tiger roared, the entire jungle became silent for few seconds. It was a wonderful experience to watch all the animals.

While roaming the zoo, Aditi noticed a deer lying on the floor in another cage. She went to have a closer look at the animal. She saw that the deer was wounded with a bleeding leg. Everybody was busy enjoying and clicking pictures that no one noticed the injured deer. Aditi immediately ran to a watchman who was standing nearby to enquire about any veterinarian in the zoo. She rushed in the direction towards the cabin where the veterinarian sat and told him about the deer. He immediately took his first aid box to the deer. The kit had few medicines, bandages, stethoscope and some other special instruments used to check animals. The veterinarian treated the deer and bandaged its wound. They called special ambulance and sent the animal a nearby animal clinic. He thanked Aditi for saving the animal. Later, that evening they went back to the hotel.

Next morning, the family was coming back to Mumbai. They reached home around 1pm. But after this trip, Aditi's heart was filled with contentment as she had an inner satisfaction of helping the needy around her. She celebrated this with a smile.

Have you ever helped someone in need?

Author

Aarav Kukreja

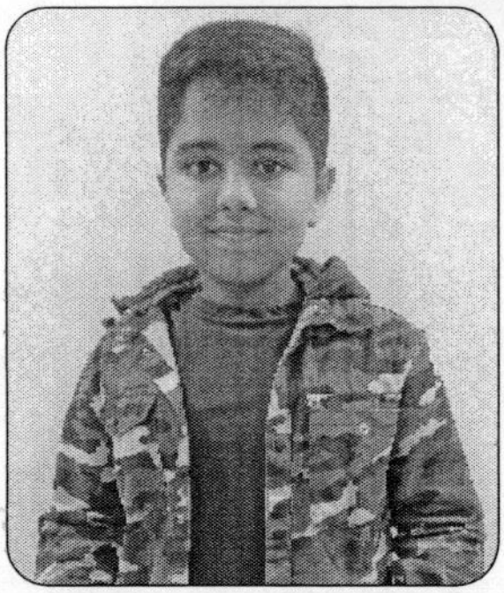

Aarav Kukreja is a 10-year old boy, born and brought up in Mumbai. His friends call him "AK". He is from St. Gregorios High School, Chembur. He is in grade 5. He loves stories related to superheroes and anti-heroes like Moonknight, Batman, Venom, and many more. The sessions that he had with Ms. Khushi Ma'am to write these two stories were marvellous. It was an amazing experience. He learned that you can do anything if you put your mind into it. It might be difficult to begin writing but once you're around the 100-word mark, ideas just keep popping into your head. His hobby is drawing. Seeing famous authors as Pranshi Mehta and Abhijita Gupta inspired him to write his own stories.

8

The Adventures of Night Blade: Part-1

By Aarav Kukreja

On a dark stormy night in a city named Anium, Dar Jake aka Flinter Steel, hid in his laboratory where he was inventing a new and stronger model of his Xs-119 flamethrower. The Xz-135 had to be a better weapon in case Night Blade showed up in the middle of his heist. Meanwhile, Night Blade was relaxed, lying in his couch watching the news.

Suddenly, the news reporter on the screen, stopped speaking about all the global politics and started talking in a worried tone, "The Anium City Central Bank (The ACCB) has been broken into by the famous crook Dar Jake. The road is blocked and the ambulance is on the way. I hope there are no casualties and that he doesn't steal anything from the vaults. There you see something happening!!!" he continued. Dar Jake went there with the sole purpose of robbing the bank. In the meanwhile, Night Blade had already left the room.

He jumped from one tower to another as fast as he could to reach the bank. Dar Jake was about to leave, when our superhero crept up without making a sound behind the villain. Dar Jake turned to check if anyone was watching him but the moment he turned Night Blade punched him hard on his face and said "Well ...Well...Well! Look who we have here." But Dar Jake cut him off, "WHY?!!! Do you always have to come at the worst time? I was almost done robbing this bank you fool!" "It's time for you to go behind bars Jake!" said Night Blade, "Nope not today Night because I have this!" he said as he showed his new and improved flamethrower the Xz-135. Night Blade kicks it out of his hand and energy blasts it into pieces. Sarcastically, Dar Jake laughed, "Ha ha ha! It is so easy to fool you Night Blade! That was a fake model, this is the real one!" he said as he showed the real Xz-135 which looked even less complex to Night Blade. He tried to kick it out of his hand again but it didn't work this time. Dar Jake quickly pulled it back and turned on the flamethrower and the heat of it quickly started to affect Night Blade but he had a trick up his sleeve. He picked up a bottle of water which was kept on a table next to him, quickly opened it and splashed it on the flamethrower and as expected it stopped the fire. "NOOOO!" screamed Dar Jake. In the meanwhile, the police already reached and immediately handcuffed and escorted him to the S.W.A.T. van which was only used for dangerous criminals. When they got him to prison, they put him in the highest security cell 40 feet underground, built with 3 feet thick titanium walls and ceiling but no floor. So when the guards were changing their shifts for the night, he plotted his plan to escape the prison. He muttered to himself in a low tone, "If I dig through the ground I have a slim chance of reaching my lab. The cops will also notice the gaping hole in the ground. What should I do?" He thought deeply and after that he fell asleep. The following night he did what he had plotted the night before. He dug down the entire time until he finally escaped. He reached his secret lab. He had accessed that lab long back. He realized there he had weapons of his failed attempts and few other spare parts of the most unique technology which were never made. He walked down the secret passageway which led to his proper lab. He put on his lab coat and started to make his base very defensive so he could hide from the cops.

Night Blade was already back at his apartment training and punching his boxing bag so hard that he almost broke the ceiling. After that near-disaster situation, he went out for a stroll at night got a snack from the bakery and as he was heading back he saw a poster with big text "WANTED, Prize 100,000 dollars" and a picture of Dar Jake. Coincidentally, at that very moment at Dar Jake's laboratory an accident occurred. A failed model exploded burning the entire lab down. Now, he realized that one: he would need a new base because this one was finished and two: he stood a chance against Night Blade.

He now changed his identity and named himself Flinter Steel. Night Blade was still hunting for him. He searched the city hoping to find him. One day, when he was walking down the lonely street he felt a hot wind all around him. He had never felt anything like that before. He realized where the heat was coming from. Someone was standing behind him and he immediately turned. It was pure fire. There was nothing on his body, except flames. It was Flinter Steel. He tried to punch him but instead his hand went through the fire. Now Flinter Steel succeeded in punching Night Blade. He fell on his knees and

Flinter Steel crackled, “This is my dream come true! To see you on my feet. HAHAHAHAHA!” But then when he looked down, Night Blade was gone.

Night Blade was running down the street looking for any place where he could find a fire extinguisher to use it on Flinter Steel. While he ran, he saw Flinter Steel coming after him, leaving a trail of fire behind. Night Blade couldn’t find anything. He had to use the dark arts, they were his final option. So, he stopped running and turned around, “I’m going to fight you Flinter Steel even if I die today!”, and with that he ran at Flinter Steel warming up a punch on his way. Now he let the dark arts loose, they swarmed around him and with one good punch, all the fire in Flinter Steel had disappeared and so had he. Now Night Blade finally could rest for a long time before the next villain showed up. At least that’s what he hoped for!

9

The Adventures of Night Blade: Part-2

By Aarav Kukreja

It was a new day in Anium City and Night Blade was fast asleep after his long battle with Flinter Steel. He was sleeping on his couch in his apartment. In another part of the city, Ethan Grake aka NightSky Zemon was constructing a new model of his Creeglinite Kama which exploded on impact. He was Dar Jake's descendent and an arch-enemy of Night Blade too. Ethan Grake was planning one of the greatest heists of his life. He was going to rob the same ACCB bank, Dar Jake had tried to rob. He would avenge him by not only robbing this bank but also by killing Night Blade if he got in his way. He went looking inconspicuous as he entered in, but as he reached his vault, he threw the tear gas cans in the bank. He took as much money as he could stuff in his gold bag. He kept his weapons ready in case Night Blade showed up, but at the same time Night Blade was at his base, hopping in his new camouflaging Mech Jet which could transform from a robot to a jet and vice versa. It was gifted by his friend named Doc Redwing.

At that moment, he was not aware that Ethan Grake was robbing the bank. When he reached home and switched on the news channel, he was surprised to watch the breaking news which flashed on the screen in bold red, 'Anium City Central bank robbed. Our hero never came'. He was so angry that he almost thrust his fist into the television. He ran into his basement and jumped into his Mech Jet and flew out, looking for the villain. Surprisingly Ethan's base was far out in the open .When Night Blade looked down, he saw a deserted warehouse which he had never seen. It had a metal board with the name 'NightSky Zemon' engraved on it. He landed on the ground and jumped out of his Mech Jet and kicked the door of the warehouse wide open. There he was, standing in a pitch black room with NightSky Zemon in the middle with what he assumed to be like bags and bags of gold coins beside him.

Suddenly he threw his Creeglinite Kama at Night Blade but missed. “Your dramatic entry will not happen in the presence of me!” said Night Blade. “Oh yeah Bladeboy!?” said NightSky Zemon sniggering. “What about an exit?” “No, won’t happen!” answered Night Blade. “Oh really?” said NightSky Zemon in a funny way. The next moment there was a cloud of smoke, a sound of distant running and a faint shout “Later loser!” Approximately after 20 minutes the fog finally cleared. Night Blade saw muddy footprints leading to the helipad and then they disappeared after a certain point.

Meanwhile NightSky Zemon was in his helicopter, noiselessly taunting him. Night Blade felt an unusually strong wind coming from above him. He looked up and saw NightSky Zemon flying away. He immediately suited up in Mech Jet and flew into the sky chasing NightSky Zemon. He came closer and caught the helicopter by its tail with his great strength. After he got a good grip onto it, Night Blade pushed it down towards the ground. The helicopter crashed on earth. The place was filled with flames and smoke. NightSky Zemon fortunately escaped the fire but was caught by the one and only Night Blade before he could vanish. “Hahaha, you will never be able to escape while I’m watching you!” “Oh! But I will” said Zemon in an odd tone and a wicked smile.

Then, he kicked Night Blade in his shin bone. His grip loosened and he ran off. “Nooooooo!” cried Night Blade, but at that very moment NightSky Zemon threw one of his Creeglinite Kamas and it exploded. “BOOM!” shouted NightSky Zemon and he was gone.

Night Blade stomped back to his jet still angry about his devastating loss. Just as he reached his house he got a brilliant plan. He thought, ‘What if I disguised myself as another weak villain trying to team up with NightSky Zemon to take down Night Blade? This would lead him into a trap.’ Would this amazing plan work? There were so many questions that were filling his mind. But now it didn’t matter. He would follow this plan to capture NightSky Zemon, no matter what. He got his shapeshifting device from his secret lab behind the wardrobe. He knew he would only get 24 hours to complete and hopefully succeed in his plan. He got into hiding near the same warehouse he had been to a couple hours ago. Then, he shape shifted into a random villain and walked in saying “Are you NightSky Zemon?” “Yes I am” replied a dull voice from the shadows, “What do you want?” “I want to help you to get revenge on Night Blade" "Deal!" NightSky said without hesitation. The plan worked flawlessly. Night Blade led him to a lab. As they entered, he said "No one knows about this lab.", he lied. "Wooooah! Said NightSky Zemon as he entered. He led him to a 'machine' which was actually a prison cell to catch hold of him. "Get into this machine to get super powers" he told NightSky Zemon "Ok, I'll get in it immediately. I am hungry for power!" As he got in, Night Blade closed the cell and locked him. "Wait, what are you doing? Why are you locking me up?" his eyes popped out when he saw Night Blade changing into his true form. "Did I trick you?" he said as he vaguely smiled and saw NightSky Zemon's face slowly filling red with anger.

He took out his Creeglinite Kama and tried to throw it but it didn't work. "Bomb proof." said Night Blade slowly. "Now that I have caught you, you will be going to—INESCAPABLE PRISON—so you can pay for what you've done." he informed a few D.C.C.G [Dangerous criminal control group] officers and left. He went back to his apartment and dozed off happily, "Another criminal down. Yay!!!"

ALL ABOUT MY SUPER-HERO

NAME

Write full name.

SPECIAL ABOUT HIM/HER

Why you like him/her.

WHAT I LOVE THE MOST

Write about qualities

CAN I BE LIKE HIM/HER

Mention Yes/No/Maybe

WHAT YOU NEED TO DO

Write about changes you need to do.

What am I celebrating today?